THE WORST
GOO IN THE WORLD

WORSE THINGS HAPPEN AT SEA!

A TALE OF
PIRATES, POISON, AND MONSTERS

by Alan Snow

OXFORD

To Issy, whose father is not very good at drawing horses
& Theo, Maya, Finn, Tom and Ruby

OXFORD
UNIVERSITY PRESS

Great Clarendon Street, Oxford OX2 6DP
Oxford University Press is a department of the University of Oxford.
It furthers the University's objective of excellence in research, scholarship,
and education by publishing worldwide in

Oxford New York

Auckland Cape Town Dar es Salaam Hong Kong Karachi
Kuala Lumpur Madrid Melbourne Mexico City Nairobi
New Delhi Shanghai Taipei Toronto

With offices in

Argentina Austria Brazil Chile Czech Republic France Greece
Guatemala Hungary Italy Japan Poland Portugal Singapore
South Korea Switzerland Thailand Turkey Ukraine Vietnam

Oxford is a registered trade mark of Oxford University Press
in the UK and in certain other countries

© Alan Snow 2011

The moral rights of the author have been asserted

Database right Oxford University Press (maker)

First published in 2010 as part of Worse Things Happen At Sea!
First published in this edition 2011

British Library Cataloguing in Publication Data

Data available

ISBN: 978-0-19-279273-0
1 3 5 7 9 10 8 6 4 2

Printed in Great Britain

Paper used in the production of this book is a natural,
recyclable product made from wood grown in sustainable forests.
The manufacturing process conforms to the environmental
regulations of the country of origin.

Contents

Johnson's Taxonomy
of Trolls and Creatures

Albatross
A true sea bird that has been known to spend up to 10 years without ever visiting land. Has large wingspan (3.5 metres). Can live up to 85 years and pairs for life.

Cabbage Island
A legendary island that is supposed to be in the southern Pacific. Said to be the home of strange plants with incredible powers. While it is not known if this island exists it is mentioned in many travelogues of the region and turns up in folklore surrounding cheese and health.

Crow
The crow is an intelligent bird, capable of living in many environments. Usually they are charming company, but should be kept from providing the entertainment. Failure to do so may result in tedium, for while intelligent, crows seem to lack taste in the choice of music, and conversational topics.

Boxtrolls
A sub-species of the common troll, they are very shy, so live inside a box. These they gather from the backs of large shops. They are somewhat troublesome creatures—as they have a passion for everything mechanical and no understanding of the concept of ownership (they steal anything which is not bolted down and, more often than not, anything which is). It is very dangerous to leave tools lying about where they might find them.

Cheese
Wild English Cheeses live in bogs. This is unlike their French cousins who live in caves. They are nervous beasties, that eat grass by night, in the meadows and woodlands. They are also of very low intelligence, and are panicked by almost anything that catches them unawares. Cheese make easy quarry for hunters, being rather easier to catch than a dead sheep.

Guillemot (paid entry)
Famously the name of the founder of the fabulous south sea trading company and mail order business. Providers of exotic and budget items for every home. Send a stamped addressed envelope and you will be amazed at just how quickly we respond (3 year delivery guaranteed).

WORSE THINGS HAPPEN AT SEA!

BOOK 2

THE WORST GOO IN THE WORLD

OXFORD

Also by Alan Snow

WORSE THINGS HAPPEN AT SEA!

HERE BE MONSTERS!

The Members
Members of the secretive Ratbridge Cheese Guild, that was thought to have died out after the 'Great Cheese Crash'. It was an evil organization that rigged the cheese market, and doctored and adulterated lactose-based food stuffs.

Legendary Monsters
Often found wandering the southern sea and should be avoided at all cost, unless you are the owner of a Guillemot Monster-repelling Kit. These are available by mail order (see entry for Guillemot). These monsters are known to reside on many islands and thought to be the last remaining dinosaurs on the planet. Last confirmed sighting—Tokyo 1723.

Grandfather (William)
Arthur's guardian and carer. Grandfather lived underground for many years in a cave home where he pursued his interests in engineering. But after some rather unusual events both Arthur and his grandfather found themselves with a new home in the former petshop now rented by Willbury Nibble and shared with boxtrolls and Titus the cabbagehead. He now wakes up late, then spends his days in the company of Willbury and all their new friends, and has been known to sneak off on his own to the Nag's Head tavern for a crafty pint and bag of pork scratchings with a pickled egg. Now relieved of the sole care of Arthur, his favourite pastime is reading in bed with his own bucket of cocoa.

Shopping Birds
A once common bird that has now become rare due to its blatant consumerism and lack of intelligence.

Rats
Rats are known to be some of the most intelligent of all rodents, and to be considerably more intelligent than many humans. They are known to have a passion for travel, and be extremely adaptable. They often live in a symbiotic relationship with humans.

Trotting Badgers
Trotting badgers are some of the nastiest creatures to be found anywhere. With their foul temper, rapid speed, and razor-sharp teeth, it cannot be stressed just how unpleasant and dangerous these creatures are. It is only their disgusting stench that gives warning of their proximity, and when smelt it is often too late.

THE STORY SO FAR ...

DIRTY WASHING

Arthur and his grandfather are on deck of the Ratbridge *Nautical Laundry*, helping their rat and pirate friends pack up piles of washing. Suddenly there is a commotion on the towpath, and they turn to see policemen and an angry mob heading straight for them. They are told that earlier that morning, the famous Countess Grogforth was insulted to see the town's underwear flying from the rigging in such a rude display.

Policemen and an angry mob

COMPENSATION

The countess was so badly shocked that she fainted away, damaging her wig. She is now seeking compensation and the town is suing for damages. Everyone on the *Nautical Laundry* is arrested and ordered to appear at court the next morning.

The damaged wig

THE STORY SO FAR

NO WAY OUT?

Now under police guard, Arthur, Grandfather, Marjorie the inventor and the rest of the crew are stuck on the ship. Grandfather knows that they must get to their friend, Willbury Nibble, a retired lawyer, who can help. Then Marjorie has the bright

She pushed up the periscope and looked about

idea to sneak away in the old submarine at the side of the ship.

CLANG!

'It looks like a bedstead.'

A collision with a bedstead in the canal leaves the submarine stuck. Marjorie manages to break it free and they arrive at Willbury's house, but Grandfather is injured by the accident.

IN THE DOCK

The next day, Willbury does his best to defend the crew—but against the crooked Judge Podger he has no chance. A hefty fine of ten thousand groats is imposed upon the *Nautical Laundry*. How on earth will they find that sum of money?

Stuffed into the dock was the entire crew

BLACK JOLLOP!

'IT WORKS!
It really works!'

Meanwhile, a Doctor I. Snook has opened a new health spa, funded by an anonymous benefactor. Ratbridge residents are clamouring for a free dose of miracle medicine 'Black Jollop', said to cure all ills. After fighting his way through the crowds, Arthur manages to get Grandfather into the spa to be cured.

AN OFFER

'TEN THOUSAND
GROATS!'

With Grandfather restored to health, everyone is surprised when the doctor turns up with some alarming news. Supplies of Black Jollop are low and a voyage to gather its secret ingredient is needed. The doctor wants Arthur and Grandfather to persuade the crew of the *Nautical Laundry* to undertake the journey for a price of ten thousand groats.

PREPARATIONS

The crew readily agree to the voyage, and Willbury is to accompany them. Arthur is devastated when he is told he is not old enough to go on the adventure, and that he must stay at home with Grandfather.

Arthur turned and walked
away down the towpath.

 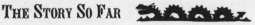

PREDATORS!

In the boggy marshes close by, the snoring of the sleeping cheeses masks the soggy footsteps of approaching predators. A baying mob, whimpering with cheese lust, is hunting them down!

Those cheeses that escaped made for the woods.

SETTING SAIL

The next morning, Marjorie entrusts the key of the submarine to a miserable Arthur for safekeeping. Seeing how unhappy Arthur is, Grandfather relents and gives his permission for Arthur to go on the journey with the *Nautical Laundry*, but when they reach the towpath, the ship has already gone!

'If you really want to go on this voyage . . . you go.'

GOING UNDER!

The little submarine started down the canal.

Reaching into his pocket for his hanky, Arthur finds the key to the submarine and realizes he can use it to catch the ship up . . . but he needs help to operate it. Fish, the boxtroll, nervously volunteers, and together they head off down the canal in pursuit.

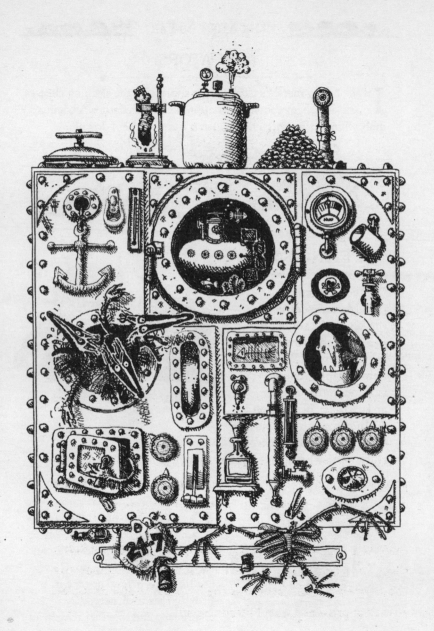

One gull tried dive-bombing the strange tube

Chapter 1

CATCHING UP

As the sun was setting over Bristol the previous evening, a few seagulls watched a periscope wander between the moored ships. One gull tried dive-bombing the strange tube, but after banging his beak on the metal, gave up and went to look for a meal elsewhere. Below the periscope Arthur and Fish were taking in turns, looking for the *Laundry*.

After a few minutes they spied the ship. Then the periscope made its way to a quiet corner of the dock and disappeared behind the hulk of an old fishing boat.

Soon two figures made their way quietly along the quayside, and up the unattended gangplank of the *Laundry*. Once on deck, Arthur looked for somewhere to hide. By the steps to the forecastle was the large barrel full of apples. Arthur approached it and lifted the lid.

'Quick Fish. Help me throw the apples over the side.'

It took the two stowaways a few minutes to make enough room to hide, but once they had, Arthur helped Fish climb into the barrel, then followed him in, and closed the lid over them. They settled themselves down amongst the last of the apples.

They settled themselves down amongst the last of the apples

'I suppose this is what it would be like in a giant squirrel's nest,' Arthur whispered to Fish.

The dim light of the moon and sound of lapping water from the dock made their way through the bunghole in the side of the barrel, and soon they were both asleep. Not even the return of the now rowdy crew awoke them, and it was only the rolling of the boat as it reached open waters that broke their slumbers.

Arthur knelt up and looked out of the bunghole

Arthur knelt up and looked out of the bunghole. Outside he could see his friends in the bright light of day. He watched Tom the rat walking past the barrel carrying a small coil of rope. Arthur was about to call out, but stopped when he remembered that they were hiding, and that until he was sure that the ship would not turn back, he'd better not reveal himself. So he made do with watching until he heard some deep rumbling and a belch behind him. He turned to see Fish breakfasting on one of the remaining apples.

'Good idea!' declared Arthur, and he grabbed an apple for himself.

For the next hour or two Fish and Arthur took turns to look out of the bunghole. Everything seemed very ordered and the rats and pirates seemed to be in their element. Arthur caught a glimpse of Willbury from time to time and then he noticed the doctor coming up to the deck from below.

Arthur watched as the doctor made his way up to the stern and spoke with Tom and Marjorie. Then Tom called out some orders and the whole crew appeared on deck. This blocked out Arthur's view. All he could see were the backs of his friends standing around the barrel.

After some more orders that Arthur couldn't make out, everybody seemed to turn towards the barrel and started counting out loud. What was happening? he wondered. Were they playing a game? The counting reached one hundred and stopped. The crew turned their backs to the barrel again and there was silence apart from a familiar voice. A small gap opened in the crowd in front of the barrel and to Arthur's horror he saw . . .

ARCHIBALD SNATCHER!

ARCHIBALD SNATCHER!

Faces turned from surprise to horror

Chapter 2

SNATCHER RETURNS!

The looks on the crew's faces turned from surprise to horror, and as they did Willbury grabbed Marjorie's arm.

'It's that awful man.'

Snatcher smiled.

'Good day my old friends. It is sooooo nice to see you all again. And how joyous it is to give you all a surprise!'

'What are you doing here?' shouted Kipper.

'Silence you squabs!' hissed Snatcher. He signalled to his men and they cocked their weapons.

'Steady now. We don't want any accidents, do we? Wouldn't want to hurt me crew.'

'What do you mean crew? We ain't your crew!' shouted Kipper.

'That I'm afraid is where you're wrong. I'm the captain now and you will address me as such!'

There was silence.

'Let me explain. The contract you signed with the doctor here gave him total control over this voyage.' He pulled the contract from his pocket and waved it in the air. 'And he decided to appoint me captain.'

He pulled the contract from his pocket and waved it in the air

The doctor, who was standing by Snatcher's side, smiled and nodded.

'My first order as captain is to have you lot demoted to "sailors third class"!'

There were gasps from the crew.

'And my second order is that all my friends here is officers.' Snatcher pointed at his evil cronies.

'Now remember, disobeying the captain or any of his officers is severely punishable.' Snatcher and his 'officers' giggled.

'He can't do this, can he?' Tom exclaimed to Willbury. 'He's a convicted criminal and criminals can't be captains. The law says so.'

Snatcher moved closer.

'Which law is that? English law? You might not have noticed but we're more than ten miles from the coast, and that means we are out of English waters and therefore English law don't apply. What does apply is international law. And under that law I'm your captain.'

'Is that true?' asked Kipper.

'Yes, I am afraid so,' replied Willbury.

'Yes indeed do!' smiled Snatcher. 'My word is law on this ship, and if I have trouble with you lot, you'll be feeling the full extent of . . . the law . . . As sailors I am sure you know disobedience can be seen as mutiny, and the punishment for mutiny is . . . ?'

The crew looked very pale.

'What's the punishment for mutiny?' muttered Marjorie.

Kipper ran his finger across his throat and made a gagging noise.

Kipper ran his finger across his throat

'Right! Want to get off on the right footing, don't we?' Snatcher jibed. 'So the crew's quarters are to be cleared for the officers, and "sailors third class" will be in the bilges. Once that's sorted I want a four course lunch, hammocks rigged up here in the sun for me and me officers, all the beer and rum to be stowed in my cabin, the entire ship scrubbed from top to toe . . . And I want a proper captain's hat—one with feathers and a big anchor on it.'

'He's power mad!' whispered Kipper.

Snatcher went on. 'I'd like lunch to be ready by one o'clock and you lot,' he said, smirking, 'will get your grub when I've decided you deserve it.'

The crew didn't move.

'Get to it! I 'eard about that cat-o'-nine-tails. Sounds like something a captain might use.'

The crew were suddenly filled with life and set about Snatcher's list. First the crew cleared their things from the crew deck and carefully lowered them through a hatch into the bilges, while the officers made themselves at home. Then hammocks were strung up. Snatcher's hammock was hung on the stern deck so he could keep an eye on things and give orders from it.

Tom found a captain's hat, decorated it with a few gull feathers and some tin foil, then presented it to the new captain.

'Ain't you got some fluffier feathers?'

'I'm afraid not.'

'Well I suppose this will have to do,' said Snatcher as he lay back in his hammock. 'Now splice the mainbrace or something!'

'Ain't you got some fluffier feathers?'

Kipper (who was at the wheel) was not quite sure what to do, but Marjorie helped him out.

'I think the captain means that you set course at full speed south, south-west.'

'Yeah. That's right,' agreed Snatcher. 'And you can bring me a compass. I don't want us going somewhere I'm not expecting.'

Marjorie provided Snatcher with a small pocket compass, then looked at the charts while Kipper set course and called for more sail.

A small pocket compass

On the main deck sailor third class Nibble was having problems. The scrubbing played hell with his knees. As he looked about to make sure nobody was watching so he could rest, he suddenly heard his name.

'Pssst . . . Mr Nibble . . . Pssst . . . Willbury . . . '

Willbury looked around and but couldn't see where the voice was coming from.

'I'm over here . . . In the barrel!'

Cautiously Willbury looked over at the barrel and saw an eye staring back at him through the bunghole. Checking that nobody was watching him he moved closer to the barrel and started to pretend to scrub the deck around it.

He moved closer to the barrel and started to pretend to scrub the deck

'Who is it?'

'Me! Arthur!'

Willbury stopped what he was doing for a moment.

'Arthur? What are you doing in there?'

'I wanted to come along. So me and Fish followed you and hid in here.'

Nervously Willbury looked about before speaking.

'You've got Fish in there as well?'

'Yes. Right cosy it is too.'

'Well, you had better just stay in there for the moment. Did you see what has just happened?'

'Yes. Snatcher! What can we do about it?'

'I am not sure there is anything we can do. But you stay hidden.'

'OK. Is there any chance you could get us some food? Both of us are rather sick of apples.'

'I will see what I can do.'

Willbury moved away from the barrel and started scrubbing his way towards Tom who was working not far away. Arthur watched as Willbury whispered to Tom.

A smile broke across Tom's face as he looked towards the barrel. Then Willbury and Tom moved around, passing on the news to their friends. In turn each of their friends took a look towards the barrel and smiled.

Over the next hour several 'sailors third class' appeared near the barrel and pushed sausages and other suitable food through the bunghole. At one point Bert appeared with a bucket and a funnel. When no one was looking Bert put the funnel through the hole and Fish and Arthur took turns to drink the water he poured through. They had been very thirsty and the water was extremely welcome, but not long after, the need to relieve themselves became overpowering. The next time Willbury came by Arthur explained the situation.

Fish and Arthur took turns to drink

'I think while lunch is being served we might be able to cause enough of a distraction to get you out for a minute.'

'Please, please do!' implored Arthur.

Lunch was delivered to Snatcher and his men, in the form of a buffet. After some words with Willbury, Tom had arranged for it to be laid out on the forecastle. Snatcher and most of his men took full advantage of it, leaving just a few officers with blunderbusses watching the main deck.

Then Arthur's friends made great play of bringing up some trays of snacks for the guards and while they were distracted, Marjorie and Bert slipped the top off the barrel and helped their friends climb out. Arthur and Fish quickly relieved themselves over the side of the ship and were helped back into the barrel.

As the lid was put back in place, Marjorie smiled at Arthur.

'Glad to have you both on board. I think we might be needing your help.'

'I think we might be needing your help.'

NOCENS SENTENTIA PRO IGNARUS

1 GROAT

THE ·Ratbridge·Gazette·

LOCAL CHEESES IN PERIL!

Late last night a frightful new attack was made on the cheeses that live just outside the town. Night-watchman Mr Ebenezer Paint (63) heard hysterical bleating at about two a.m. as he performed his duties.

'I was just brewing up a cuppa on the town wall when I heard a right pitiful noise. So I had a quick look and was shocked. There was a crowd of maniacs chasing some poor cheeses across the fields.'

Mr Paint (97) told of the horrific scenes of carnage as the mob caught up with the cheeses. 'It was horrid. I never want to see anything like that ever again! They descended on 'em like beasts. Terrible it were!'

'When it was over the mob came back towards the town, and after seeing what they did to them cheeses I hid meself.'

Later Mr Paint (14) summoned the police and led them to the crime scene.

'It were not a sight for those with a weak disposition,' reported a police spokesperson.

After cordoning off the crime scene a search was made for the offenders, but none were apprehended.

This paper is outraged that such a thing could happen twice within a week. We have to stop it! To this end we are now going to offer a reward of twenty-five groats for information leading to a conviction of these criminals (terms and conditions apply).

Marjorie took out all the maps

Chapter 3

SAIL AND STEAM

After lunch the doctor gave Marjorie a small piece of paper with a map reading on it.

'This is where we're heading.'

Marjorie took out all the maps that were kept in a locker by the wheel, and after spending quite a lot of time studying them she spoke.

'Are you sure this is right? This reading gives the position of a small island in the Pacific!'

'Is that a problem for you?' Snatcher snapped.

'It's halfway round the world!'

'And your point is?'

Marjorie looked up at Kipper and shook her head. 'It's a long, long way. Have you ever sailed that far?'

Kipper shook his head.

'Well, you better get to it then,' smiled Snatcher.

'It could take months. I doubt we have enough provisions for a journey like that.'

'Well, you better work out how we can get there fast then. One thing you can bet on is it ain't going to be me and me officers who go short.'

Marjorie gave Kipper a worried look.

'Do you mind if I call a meeting? I'll have to organize things if we're to speed this journey up.'

'All right, but I will be keeping a very close eye on yer. Don't want no funny business.'

Marjorie called the crew on deck.

'Our captain is asking us to sail to the Southern Pacific.'

This was met by silence.

'If we're to make it before the food runs out we're going to have to use steam. I want half the crew to work the sails and the other half stoking the boiler.'

'Hang on a minute,' snapped Snatcher from his hammock. 'Leave us a cook. I want me grub.'

'Hang on a minute.'

'Very well. So apart from the cook I want you divided in two. We'll work shifts and get going as fast as we can.'

Two teams formed and soon the boiler was back in action. Once the steam was up the ship started surging forward and Marjorie took several readings over the course of the next few hours. Using these calculations she tried to work out if they would make it before running out of food and fuel.

'I reckon it's going to be a very tight thing,' she muttered to Kipper. 'If we have any hold ups we're done for, and the last part of the journey will have to be under sail as we'll have run out of fuel by then.'

'Can't we stop somewhere and get some more?' asked Kipper.

'I can't see Snatcher wanting us to stop off. Might give us a chance to escape.'

'If we are going to the South Pacific, does that mean we have to go around the Cape?'

'Yes . . . yes it does.'

Kipper looked worried.

'Not sure the ship will stand up to that.'

'It will have to.'

The ship forged ahead. Even though all the crew were now very worried by the voyage, they could not help but somewhat enjoy the feeling of the ship travelling at high speed. Snatcher loved the speed and soon went to the forecastle to watch the waves crash on the bows.

Kipper turned to Marjorie.

The ship forged ahead

'The ship is going well.'

'Yes. We might even make it.'

'Do you think that's a good thing?'

'Why?'

'Have you asked yourself why Snatcher would want to go somewhere to collect something to make medicine to give away?'

'No . . . I wonder what he is up to?'

'So do I.'

'You can bet we don't know the full story.'

'Yes, but I just can't work it out.'

For the rest of the day Snatcher wandered about giving pointless orders, and finally asked for supper. He seemed so happy with the way things were going that he offered the crew food.

'I think even the sailors third class might deserve a crumb. When me and me officers have finished and the washing up is done I think I might allow them a light supper. Let them break open the hardtack.'

'What's hardtack?' asked one of the officers.

'It's ship's biscuits.'

'Sounds nice.'

Kipper, who was still at the wheel, didn't look happy at the prospect.

'More like lumps of rock with worms in. We only keep them for emergencies on long voyages. They are so hard you have to soak them just to be able to scrape off a layer with your teeth.'

'But I understand they really are very nutritious,' giggled Snatcher.

'More like lumps of rock with worms in'

As the sun went down supper was served for Snatcher and his men and after it an order was given to move all food apart from the hardtack to the captain's cabin. The crew were unhappy but with blunderbusses being waved around, the stores were soon stowed in Snatcher's quarters.

Then a large wooden crate of biscuits was brought up on deck.

'Here's your rations. I am giving you the lot. If you run out then it's your bad luck so I suggest you keep some back.'

A little more edible…

The crew took some biscuits and used mugs of lukewarm water to soak them in to try to make them a little more edible. After just about getting them down, those who were on the overnight watch settled to their tasks while the rest of the crew were locked in the bilges and tried to get some sleep. This was difficult as there was water slopping about and the soap that was left over from when the bilges had been used for laundry now created mountains of frothy damp foam.

'At least it is clean,' muttered Willbury.

'At least it is clean'

On the night watch Tom was in charge of the wheel. Between taking their position from the stars and steering he kept a watchful eye on the barrel. Around midnight the officers had cocoa and wandered up to the forecastle leaving Tom alone. Quickly he tied the wheel in position and crept down on deck to the barrel.

'Arthur!' he whispered. 'It's safe. The guards aren't looking. If you need to get out and . . . you know what . . .'

The top of the barrel lifted and out popped Arthur and Fish's heads.

Out popped Arthur's and Fish's heads

'It's good to get some fresh air,' whispered Arthur.

Tom pointed up to the forecastle with one hand and put a finger to his lips with the other. Arthur and Fish climbed out of the barrel, and had a quick stretch in the shadows before Tom signalled to them to follow him to the store cabin under the forecastle. Once inside he spoke.

'This is blooming awful. Snatcher has taken control of the food and there doesn't seem to be much we can do about it.'

'Do you know what Snatcher is up to?' asked Arthur.

'No. We've all been trying to work it out. Got to be something dodgy. Snatcher never does anything for anyone unless there is a lot in it for Snatcher.'

'I hope we find out before it is too late.'

Footsteps creaked on the boards of the deck above them and Tom signalled them back to the barrel.

'I've got a little something for you to make life more comfortable.' Tom handed Arthur something small wrapped in a hanky, before closing the lid over his friends.

Tom handed Arthur something small wrapped in a hanky

'Captain . . .'

Chapter 4

PARTY PLAN

For the next few days the ship sped towards the South Atlantic. With the combination of steam and sail it was only going to be a few days before they reached the Equator.

Bert had an idea. Without telling the others he approached Snatcher.

'Captain . . . '

'Yes?'

'Did you know that it is traditional to have a party when you cross the Equator?'

Snatcher looked very doubtful. 'Why would I want to hold a party for scum?'

'It wouldn't be for us, sir. No, it's just to honour the captain and for a bit of fun.'

Snatcher was intrigued. 'Is it indeed? Tell me more.'

'Well it involves you and an assistant dressing up. You

as Neptune, the king of the sea, and your assistant as a mermaid.'

'A mermaid!' Snatcher looked surprised. 'And then what?'

'Well, everybody has to come on deck and you have to punish any officer who has never been across the Equator for any crimes they might have committed.'

Neptune with assistant mermaid

'This is starting to sound fun. And how do I punish these miscreants?'

'Nothing too nasty. Usually a large tub of goo is made up from anything we can find around the ship. You have a big brush and splat it on them!'

A smile spread over Snatcher's face. The idea appealed.

'This sounds like a tradition I might like to carry on,' said Snatcher, mulling it over. 'But I do think it's pretty cheeky of you to come here and ask me to splat my own men . . .'

Bert looked a little worried—until Snatcher gave him a

wink. 'But this is too good an opportunity to miss out on. So when do we get to the equator?'

'Late tomorrow at this rate.'

There were several officers sitting with Snatcher, and they were now looking daggers at Bert.

They were now looking daggers at Bert

'If it is to be done properly, you'll arrive on deck as Neptune about ten minutes before we cross the Equator— with your mermaid assistant.'

'And let me guess . . . You lot get to watch me goo my officers?'

Bert tried not to look happy at this.

'Very well, I shall do it,' said Snatcher. 'You're in charge of getting the goo and costumes ready.'

'Yes, captain!' said Bert, saluting. 'And who'll be the mermaid? I'll need to know so the costume fits.'

Snatcher thought for a minute. 'I think my friend the doctor would do.'

The doctor, who'd been listening, started to protest.

'No, please not me.'

'It is either that or being punished for disobeying orders!'

'What's the goo made of?'

'Given what we have to hand I think bilge water, treacle, old oil, glue . . . That sort of stuff.'

The officers looked outraged and more than somewhat worried.

'All right. A merman I shall be.'

'Mermaid,' Snatcher corrected him.

'Very well. A mermaid.'

'By the way, what does this Neptune bloke wear?' asked Snatcher.

'A crown of shells and a cloak. Sort of fishy theme. It'll be very elegant.'

'Well just you make sure it's not too fishy, or I'll be doing some punishing of whoever's responsible.'

'Would my costume be very fishy?' asked the doctor.

'Mermaids is fish!' answered Snatcher. 'So I think fishy is the very soul of your costume.'

Bert snapped a salute. 'I shall get right to it then, captain!'

'I shall get right to it then, captain!'

NOCENS SENTENTIA PRO IGNARUS

1 GROAT

THE ·Ratbridge·Gazette·

RECOVERED TENNIS ELBOW SUFFERER FOUND IN POSSESSION OF CHEESY MORSELS!

At daybreak today one of our reporters accompanied the local constabulary in the raid that apprehended a suspected member of the mob that has been carrying out the recent cheese outrages. At 6.47 a.m. police raided the dwellings of Mrs J. Topperthwaite after a tip-off, and there discovered cheesy morsels hidden in a sofa.

The anonymous information was supplied by Ms Maya Singer (a cleaning lady), who suspected her employer of 'cheese eating' after finding scatterings of fermented lactose while cleaning Mrs Topperthwaite's drawing room.

'I couldn't believe it! She seemed such a nice old dear, but once I found the crumbs of cheese I knew it were my duty to report her. Do I get the reward now?'

Mrs Topperthwaite is now in custody. After her foul feast of cheese we hope she gets dished up her 'just desserts'!

It did actually look quite good

Chapter 5

A BARREL OF FUN?

In spare moments from their other duties the 'sailors third class' set about work on the costumes and goo. Snatcher gave them permission to search the ship (apart from his cabin) for anything they needed, and the crew took full advantage. Although officers were sent to watch the search, they were careful not to cause any problems in case it made Snatcher unhappy. The officers were already worried about any crimes they might have committed that Snatcher might use against them.

The next day around teatime Bert delivered the costumes and told Snatcher that they would be crossing the Equator at about 8.30 p.m.

'I see you have been hard at work,' Snatcher said as he admired his Neptune outfit, then he put it on. It did actually look quite good. The crown of shells looked rather regal in a shabby sort of way.

Snatcher turned his attention to the mermaid costume. 'My darling doctor, you're going to look like the most beautiful . . . fish.'

Then, eyeing up the costume, Snatcher asked, 'Do mermaids have legs?'

'Do mermaids have legs?'

'Not really,' said Bert. 'Just a tail. But we gave the costume legs so that the doctor would be able to walk.'

'Stitch the legs together!' ordered Snatcher.

Bert set off with the costume under his arm and a smile on his face. He soon returned with the costume altered as Snatcher had asked. Snatcher took a good look and then spoke.

'Good! Doctor, would you like to go and change? I can't wait to see how my Mer-assistant is going to look.'

'Very good . . . ' the doctor mumbled as he went off holding the costume.

'Now, how is the goo?'

'Would you like to come and inspect it, captain?'

'Yes please. I don't want any sub-standard goo.'

Bert led Snatcher to the main deck where a large half-barrel stood, covered by a sheet. Bert whipped the sheet off and Snatcher pulled back as the smell hit him.

'What's in it?'

'Lots of things,' said Bert.

'Not too lethal, I hope.'

'I don't think there is anything in there that would kill anyone,' said Bert.

Bert whipped the sheet off

'Smells a bit?'

'Is a bit not enough?'

Snatcher smiled. 'Is it possible to make it smellier?'

'Certainly!'

'Well, get to it then!'

Bert thought for a moment, then grinned.

'Bert? What are you going to use?' asked Tom.

Bert had a twinkle in his eye. 'Wait and see!'

With that he set off across the deck to where the trotting badgers that Snatcher had brought along were being kept in a large crate.

'What do trotting badgers produce that is very, very smelly?' called Bert as he stood by the crate.

'You can't be serious?' said Tom.

'Get me a metal spade,' giggled Bert as he pulled something from his pocket.

'What you got there?' asked Tom.

'Hardtack!'

He waved the biscuit in the air. Suddenly the trotting badgers' noses pricked up and they ran to the barred front of their shelter. Tom handed Bert a spade while the officer looked on in horror.

'Watch this.'

Bert threw the hardtack into the back of the crate and the badgers descended upon it. Quick as a flash Bert then slipped the spade under the bars and scooped up something from the floor, then withdrew the spade.

Bert slipped the spade under the bars

Then Bert walked back to the tub of goo and tipped whatever was on the spade into the goo.

'DISGUSTING!' moaned the crew.

There was silence from the officers.

The goo tub

Then Neptune appeared

Chapter 6

THE KING AND QUEEN OF THE OCEANS

At eight-twenty Marjorie took a reading on the sextant and declared they were about to reach the Equator. The ship's bell was rung and the officers reluctantly assembled on deck, while the crew arranged themselves on the forecastle to get a good view. Then Neptune appeared.

Arthur, who had been keeping tabs on things from inside the barrel, was quite impressed with the way Snatcher looked.

'Here, have a look, Fish. This isn't something you'll see every day.' And he moved around the barrel so his friend could view what was happening.

The officers stared at their leader.

Then there was a lot of clonking and swearing and a

mermaid flopped out of the doorway from the stairs and fell flat on the deck. The poor doctor was wearing the tail, a pair of coconuts as a bikini top, and a long wig made from seaweed. He was not happy as he tried to stand up, and moved like a beached seal. Snatcher on the other hand seemed jollier than the crew had ever seen him before. He walked up to the goo tub and raised an old broom he'd been clutching.

A mermaid flopped out of the doorway from the stairs and fell flat on the deck

'Bow before the King of the Sea,' he ordered. Everyone did as they were told.

'I am Neptune, King of the Seven Seas, and I have risen from my kingdom to dish out punishment to those who deserve it!'

The 'sailors third class' smiled and the officers started shaking nervously. Snatcher then took out a list from under his cloak and began to read.

'I have decided that each punishment shall fit each crime.' Snatcher scanned the officers to find his first victim before turning his eyes back to the list.

'Gristle! You are guilty of the crime of darning my socks with wire. This is unforgivable and has played havoc with my bunions. Therefore I call you to stand before me, and remove your footwear!'

Gristle came forward. He looked a little puzzled, but took off his shoes and socks.

'Right then. Do your worst!' Gristle said with something approaching defiance.

'Oh I will Gristle. I will!' And Snatcher dipped the broom into the barrel.

The broom broke a thin crust on top of the goo. As the smell hit Gristle he almost fell over. Something chemically horrid had happened to the brew.

'Please . . . no!' said Gristle, backing off.

'If you run away, you'll only make it worse for yourself. I shall be forced to give you a double ration!' warned Snatcher.

Gristle froze.

'I anoint you in the name of Neptune!' intoned Snatcher and he took the goo-laden broom and slowly slopped it onto Gristle's feet. The goo settled like thick treacle on a pudding.

'It terrible, but I can't believe how satisfying it was to watch the appalling man get daubed,' Willbury muttered to Marjorie.

'You are now anointed,' Snatcher proclaimed with a satisfied grin. 'Next please!'

Gristle unstuck himself from the deck, and glooped his way back to his place amongst the officers, but found that a large space cleared around him.

Snatcher handed the list to his mermaid.

The mermaid studied the list and looked a little puzzled.

Gristle unstuck himself from the deck

'It says here "Ernest Grunge found guilty of F.O.B."?'

'Yes!' replied Snatcher. 'Fingers on bacon. I noticed his thieving hands disappearing with a rasher I was after at breakfast.'

Fingers on bacon

A space now cleared around the unfortunate Ernest Grunge. 'I didn't know you wanted that bacon!'

'You is bleedin' common. Didn't your mother tell you to ask before grabbin' the last rasher?'

Grunge shook his head.

'So you need an education then. Roll back your sleeves!' ordered Snatcher.

Grunge crept forward, rolling back his shirtsleeves.

'Hold them out!'

Grunge did as he was told. Snatcher dipped the broom in the goo, and slapped it on the outstretched hands.

'Yuck!' whispered Bert with rather more glee than might be considered polite.

'Grunge, you are now anointed. Who's next?'

'Let's see . . . "Lardwell Fruitfly. N.I.B."'

'Ah yes! My dear Lardwell, I saw you sneaking a look at some of my papers.'

Poor Lardwell Fruitfly looked perplexed. 'I'm sorry, Guv! I was only tidying things up.'

'Well, that is not how it looked to me,' snapped Snatcher.

'Errrr . . . what does N.I.B. stand for?'

'Nose in business! Can you guess what is going to happen next?'

Lardwell looked horrified and started to back away.

'Grab him!'

Two officers grabbed him and pushed him forward.

There was a swish, then a splat, and Lardwell's prominent nose was hidden under a thick coating of goo. As the fumes hit him he fainted.

There was a swish, then a splat, and Lardwell's prominent nose was hidden under a thick coating of goo

'Next!' called Snatcher.

Neptune's mermaid was starting to enjoy this, and read off the next entry.

'"Fingle. T.I.J."'

'Ooo! Fingle. You bad lad! Can you guess what T.I.J. stands for?'

'No, but I promise I'll not do it again if you let me off.'

'That may be so but I still think you would benefit from the lesson. So . . . T.I.J?'

Fingle just slowly shook his head.

'Tongue in jam!'

Fingle went white. 'You are not going to put that stuff on my tongue are you?'

'Fingle, you know the punishment has to fit the crime.'

Fingle made a bolt for the mast.

'Get him!' shouted Snatcher.

Fingle managed to reach the mast and shin up the first nine feet before the officers reached its base.

Fingle managed to reach the mast

'OK. Leave him,' snorted Snatcher. 'He'll have to come down . . . and when he does . . . Mermaid, next on the list, please.'

Snatcher worked his way down the list and all the officers apart from Fingle got their just comeuppance. Then Neptune retired happily to the captain's cabin for a nightcap and the crew were given the job of hosing down the punished. There was a pump used to clean out the bilges and this was easily adapted for the purpose. Kipper took charge.

'Right then. All of you who want a wash, hold on to the mast with your dirty bits pointed outwards.'

The officers braced themselves and Kipper had the best fifteen minutes of fun of his life, while the crew cheered and watched with glee. By the time the officers were clean, most had very few clothes remaining and those clothes that did remain were in tatters.

Kipper had the best fifteen minutes of fun of his life

'Shall I wash out the tub?' Kipper asked.

'I think it is Snatcher's idea that we keep that back for Fingle. Just nail down a lid on it to keep the smell down,' Tom suggested.

A lid was made and it was decided to throw the broom over the side. A few hours later dead fish could be found floating in the wake of the ship.

A few hours later dead fish could be found floating in the wake of the ship

NOCENS SENTENTIA PRO IGNARUS

1 GROAT

THE ·Ratbridge·Gazette·

CHEESE SURVIVAL THREATENED IN FURTHER ATTACKS

'After the recent appalling attacks there has been a noticeable decline in cheese numbers. If there are any more losses, our cheeses may not have a large enough breeding population to survive and they could become extinct!' reported Cuthbert Milk, chairman of the Ratbridge Wildlife Conservation Association.

This shocking revelation comes in the shadow of yet another outrage. Only last night police tried to arrest 'Cheesy Crims' returning to the town after another dastardly attack. Unfortunately the police were overpowered and the mob escaped.

These outrages must stop. This paper will now raise the reward for the capture of 'Cheesy Crims' to 100 groats.

Arthur put a leg over the edge of the barrel and lifted himself out

Chapter 7

THE NIGHT WATCH

Arthur and Fish had taken it in turns to enjoy the entertainment, and now things had quietened down Arthur's mind had turned to food. That morning they had finally run out of apples and the ship's biscuits that Tom had sneaked in to them were horrid.

'We have to get something else to eat.'

Outside, the crew on the night watch were busy and Arthur was unable to catch anyone's attention.

'Right Fish. I think we are on our own.' After a quick look out of the bunghole Arthur lifted the lid and looked about. With ripped and sodden clothes, the officers who were supposed to be on guard were huddled by the boiler trying to keep warm.

Arthur put a leg over the edge of the barrel and lifted himself out. Fish followed.

'If we make our way round to the other side of the deck we can get down the stairs and might be able to find something,' Arthur whispered.

They crept across the deck and made their way towards the steps leading to the deck below. As they reached the top of the steps, there was a sudden shout from somewhere above.

'Oi, down there. Someone is creeping about!' It was Fingle. He was still up the mast for fear of what might happen if he came down.

'Oi, down there. Someone is creeping about!'

The guards looked up but couldn't see Arthur and Fish as the beam engine was in the way.

'Where are they?'

'By the steps to the cabins.'

Arthur and Fish had stopped in their tracks.

'Quick, Fish. Back to the barrel.'

The officers jumped up and drew their blunderbusses.
'FIND THEM!'

A couple of officers ran to the top of the stairway and then turned back to catch the sight of Arthur and Fish running away. A few of the crew members on deck started moving to block the officers' way, but in an instant guns were trained on them and they were ordered not to move.

Arthur reached the front end of the deck and could see there was nowhere to go apart from the forecastle. He and Fish ran up the steps. At the top he turned. The first of the guards was approaching the steps behind them so he took a loose pulley block and threw it.

'Youch!'

'Youch!'

The officer stopped as the block bounced off his head. Then he made for the steps again. Arthur threw another block. Again it found its target and the officer pulled back.

'Get the crew below, then I need you all over here to help me deal with this boy and his friend.'

The other officer did as he was told and, with the aid of his blunderbuss, marched the crew below and locked them in the bilges. Then he returned with reinforcements. Arthur could see that the net was closing in on him.

'What are we going to do?' he nervously asked Fish.

Fish gave no answer so Arthur picked up another pulley block, and Fish followed his lead. Seeing them making ready to throw, the officers ran and hid behind the trotting badger crate.

'You put those down, or we'll fire!' came a shout from behind the crate.

Arthur and Fish looked at each other, then turned and threw the blocks as hard as they could in the direction of the shout, then dropped to the ground.

There was a loud crash, an outbreak of snarling from the trotting badgers, and a return of fire. After a few shots the firing stopped as the officers reloaded.

Arthur and Fish stood again, took careful aim and threw two more blocks in the direction of the crate before diving for cover.

Again there was crashing from the direction of the crate, but this time it was followed by screams.

'Must have hit them!' smiled Arthur.

They waited for a few seconds for more gunfire but the screams grew louder and shots didn't come.

Arthur inched his way to the edge of the forecastle and looked over.

The blocks that Arthur and Fish had thrown had done their work but not in the way he had expected. The crate was shattered and the officers were now fending off an attack from the vicious creatures. All the noise and excitement had wound the badgers to a new level of anger, and they were expressing this anger with their jaws

A new level of anger

The officers fought to escape and slowly managed to reach the door to the stairwell. The effect of them all trying to get through the door at the same time was a blockage.

The badgers saw their chance and pounced. Teeth sank again and again into flesh and tattered trouser. At the front of the blockage in the stairwell one man manage to loosen himself, and pulled free. This had a dramatic effect. Like a cork the blockage popped out and Snatcher's men tumbled down the stairs. The badgers stopped for a moment in surprise, then followed.

Then the badgers saw their chance and pounced

The screaming heap now filled the corridor outside the Captain's cabin.

'Let us in,' screamed one of the officers.

The door opened, and Snatcher was knocked to the ground by the officers, who then scrambled over him. As he sat up he saw the maddened trotting badgers careering along the corridor towards him. With a swift kick of the foot he slammed the door and pushed both of his feet against it. Then a great thump made the door shudder.

'Fetch the desk, blast you!' Snatcher screamed at his men.

Somewhere above, Arthur smiled at Fish.

'I think we'd better block off the top of the stairwell or those badgers will be able to get us.'

They rushed down and across the deck and threw shut the very heavy storm doors that closed off the stairwell. Then Arthur flipped the large iron latch across.

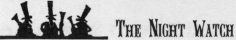

'That's it! We trap the badgers, and the badgers trap Snatcher and his mob! Now what do we do?'

Fish gave a happy gurgle.

'Go and free the others?'

Fish nodded, and they made their way across the deck and down through the forward hatch to the crew deck.

At the end of the crew deck towards the stern was a doorway to the corridor where the badgers were trapped. Fortunately it was closed. Arthur tiptoed towards it, listening to the awful sounds coming from the other side, then turned the key in the lock.

Then they opened the hatch to the bilges.

'Anybody want to go for a walk?'

The eyes of their friends stared up at them.

'Arthur. What has happened?'

'Anybody want to go for a walk?'

'Fish and I have sorted everything out. We've taken over the ship and locked Snatcher and his mob in the captain's cabin. I hope you don't mind.'

After a few seconds of stunned silence came a huge joyful shout.

'HOORAY!'

'Come on. I think it's time for us to have our own Equator party.'

It didn't take long for the crew to make their way on deck and start celebrating their freedom.

'I don't know how you did it, but I'm glad you're here.' Arthur turned to see Willbury smiling at him and looking a little embarrassed.

'But you . . . '

'I was only thinking of your best interests.'

These now shook from the impact of the trotting badgers

While the crew partied on deck, below, Snatcher and his men had managed to stack the desk and several large sea

chests against the door. These now shook from the impact of the trotting badgers.

Snatcher looked about. 'This could have gone better.'

'Pity we don't have any Black Jollop to fix the wounds,' said the doctor.

'Yes. But even I wouldn't poison my men with that stuff.'

Breakfast had been hardtack and a few small fish

Chapter 8

FREEDOM

'What are we going to do about Snatcher and his mob?' asked Tom the following morning. 'And are we just going to turn around and go home now?'

'And what about food?' added Kipper. Breakfast had been hardtack and a few small fish that the crew had managed to catch over the side.

'I think we might be able to do some negotiation on the food front,' replied Marjorie. 'They're going to be stuck in that cabin until we help them out so I think we hold most of the cards.'

'Yes, I wonder what they'll be prepared to pay for removal of the trotting badgers?' giggled Kipper.

'I don't think totally removing the trotting badgers is our best bet,' smirked Bert. 'I think that just removal of the immediate threat of a good chewing is enough to get us what we want.'

'Sounds like a good idea. Follow me!' Marjorie led the crew up on to the bridge and leant over the stern.

With a boathook she knocked on the window of the captain's cabin, and after a few seconds the window opened and Snatcher's head popped out.

She knocked on the window of the captain's cabin

'Good morning!' smiled Marjorie.

'Get us out of here!' Snatcher yelled. 'That is an order.'

'Pardon me,' said Marjorie. 'What did you say?'

'I said get us out of here. AND THAT IS AN ORDER!' repeated Snatcher. 'If you don't I shall have you all for mutiny!'

'I am very sorry,' apologized Marjorie. 'But I am afraid we can't hear you.'

The crew all laughed.

'Will you *please* get us out of here,' Snatcher asked, a little more politely.

'I don't think we can,' said Bert. 'The trotting badgers might attack us if we tried. And you wouldn't want any of your crew injured, would you?'

'I just might . . . ' muttered Snatcher under his breath. Then he spoke louder. 'So what are you expecting us to do? Stay in here for the rest of the trip?'

'I should say that is a distinct possibility,' said Marjorie.

'Can't you lower a rope ladder and let us climb out? Please?'

'That might also be dangerous. We wouldn't want any of you falling in the sea,' said Marjorie. 'I think it best for everybody if you stay where you are.'

'Blow you! Are you just going to leave us here? Those trotting badgers could break through any time.'

'Those trotting badgers could break through any time'

'Well I think things can be organized properly to stop that happening,' replied Marjorie.

'How do you mean?' snapped Snatcher.

'Well, it would be very inconvenient for the captain to be stuck in the cabin during the rest of the trip. It might be better for him to be on deck with his crew.'

'I couldn't agree with you more!' said Snatcher, looking a little happier.

'Well, as you agree, and are stuck down there, I suggest you appoint a new captain.'

'Blowed if I will!' Snatcher was furious at the suggestion.

'Well, without the correct orders the crew might not be able to help protect you from those vicious badgers,' Marjorie said with a smile.

'I will not be pushed around by a . . . WOMAN! Get me out of here at once!'

'I am sorry. I didn't hear you.' Then Marjorie turned to the rest of the crew who were watching. 'Did any of you hear anything?'

The crew all shook their heads, and laughed.

Arthur smiled and waved to his friends to come close. 'I have an idea that might help.'

'What would that be?' asked Willbury.

'It's a little bit naughty, but I think it'll help Snatcher come round to our way of thinking.'

'Well in the circumstances, anything "a little bit naughty" might be all right. What is it?'

'Watch!' said Arthur. Then he crossed the stern deck and went down the steps to the locked doorway.

The crew watched as Arthur raised his fists and started banging them on the doors.

'WAKEY, WAKEY, badgers! WAKEY, WAKEY!'

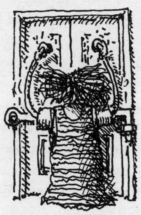

'WAKEY, WAKEY, badgers!'

This seemed to do the trick. There was a flurry of snarling and banging from below deck, followed by screams of fear from the captain's cabin.

The crew rushed back to the stern rail to see what would happen.

Snatcher's head popped out of the cabin window and he started yelling.

'Quick! They're breaking through!'

'It will cost you.'

'What?'

There was some more banging and screaming from below and Snatcher looked nervously back into the cabin.

'What do you want?'

'Half the food.'

'Never!'

'Half the food!'

'NO!'

'Well then, enjoy yourselves with your furry little friends,' Kipper called down.

Snatcher looked panicked. 'OK, OK! But what do I get in return?'

'How about some metal sheeting, a hammer, and nails?'

'Perfect! Lower it down quick and I'll send up the food.'

'I think we both know who's to be trusted around here,' said Marjorie. 'You send up the food, and then we'll send down the metal sheet and tools.'

'OK! OK! Just send down a rope.'

Marjorie leant over and whispered in Kipper's ear. 'Tell Arthur to bang on the door some more.'

Marjorie spoke again as Kipper disappeared. 'We need to sort out this captain thing.'

Snatcher was about to reply when the noise of badgers and screams started up again.

'Would you like to appoint my friend Tom as captain so he can get the rope organized?'

A nervous Snatcher nodded.

'All right, I appoint that rat Tom captain.'

A rope was lowered with a large net on the end and very quickly the food was loaded. Then, as promised, a sheet of tin, some nails, and a hammer were sent down in exchange. While Snatcher and his mob nailed the metal up, the crew had their first good meal in days.

As they ate they discussed what to do next. No one was quite sure; but soon they would have their minds made up for them.

Then, as promised, a sheet of tin, some nails,
and a hammer were sent down in exchange

NOGENS SENTENTIA PRO IGNARUS

1 GROAT

·THE· Ratbridge·Gazette·

POLICE BRING IN HOUNDS TO CATCH CHEESY CRIMS

In an attempt to track down the perpetrators of the ongoing cheese outrages, a number of cheese-hounds have been purchased from the Ratbridge Holiday Home for Cats and Dogs, and Economy Pie Company. The hounds are being used because they have a keen sense of smell and a strong desire for  cheese. Already the dogs have helped to close the net on the Cheesy Crims. Yesterday afternoon seventeen people were arrested after the hounds tracked the scent to various addresses in the town.

In one surprising raid, the Honourable Mr Clifford Swage (Mayor of Ratbridge) was detained. This paper says 'Let justice be done. No one is above the law!'

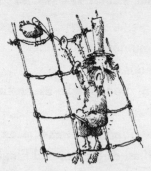

He was cold, hungry, and his bottom had a painful groove in it

Chapter 9

THE BIG SECRET

Fingle had had enough of watching life from up in the rigging. He was cold, hungry, and his bottom had a painful groove in it where he'd been sitting on a rope. Giving himself up to the crew couldn't be much worse. So he climbed down and presented himself to Bert and a couple of the larger pirates.

'What shall we do with this sneak? He's the one that almost got Arthur caught. Shall I rough him up?' Bert was straining at the leash.

'We'll have none of that.' Willbury had appeared with Arthur by his side. 'I think he might answer a few questions though.'

'What do you want to know?' asked the dishevelled Fingle.

'Some information about Black Jollop, this trip, and what Snatcher is up to with the doctor.'

'I ain't telling you nothin'.'

'When did you last eat?'

'Days ago . . . ' said Fingle, as he held his shrunken stomach.

'Bert, could you bring me a fresh bacon sandwich?'

'Is that for me?' asked the hopeful Fingle.

'It might be, but then again I might fancy it, or perhaps Bert would.'

'Yup! I fancy a bacon sandwich all right. A nice thick one with loads of ketchup and butter.'

There was an odd empty gurgling sound from Fingle's stomach.

Bert smiled slyly at hearing the noise. 'As I remember there is only enough bacon left for one really good sandwich. I do feel quite peckish, but bacon makes such good fishing bait. Maybe we should just throw it over the side instead?'

'Stop it! This is cruel and unusual punishment, this is! Blooming torture!'

'To you it may be torture, but to me it is just a sandwich. I can take it or leave it. Actually I don't know if I fancy one really, maybe I'll just throw it over the side.'

'Stop it! This is cruel and unusual punishment, this is!'

 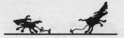

'You're mad, and cruel!' Fingle looked very worried. 'What do you want to know?'

The retired lawyer stood and took hold of his lapels.

'I want to know about the Black Jollop. Are the effects permanent?'

'As far as I know,' stuttered Fingle.

'And why would Archibald Snatcher be behind a scheme to hand out free medicine to the people of Ratbridge?'

Fingle started to twitch nervously. 'It's more than my life's worth to tell yer.'

The sandwich arrived and Fingle's eyes fell upon it.

Willbury took the sandwich and sniffed it. 'Very nice. Finest Gloucester Old Spot, I think?'

'Finest Gloucester Old Spot, I think?'

'Correct, Mr Nibble. The bread is just out of the oven, and I think they've used un-salted Danish butter,' Bert added.

The saliva was starting to run down Fingle's chin.

'You can't do this to me. I, I, I . . . If I tells yer, yer promise me yer won't put me back with Snatcher?'

'If you don't tell me what I want to know I will put you back with him. And I might just thank you in front of him for telling me about the Black Jollop even if you haven't.'

Fingle went white.

'Whereas if you tell me everything I just might let you have a couple of rounds of fat juicy bacon sandwiches.'

'What do you want to know?'

'So, the Black Jollop?'

'It's poison.'

Everybody but Fingle looked shocked. 'Can I have a bite now?'

'No, not yet. What on earth do you mean "it's poison"? We've all seen it cure people!'

'Well, it does cure things. Loads of things. But there's a downside.'

'What downside?' snapped Willbury.

'It has effects. Right interesting ones. And I ain't telling you more until I get a bite.'

'Very well.' Willbury held out the sandwich and two large pirates holding Fingle let him lean forward to take a bite.

'Tell me more or that will be the last of the sandwich you taste.'

Fingle quickly swallowed, and spoke again.

'It's the cheese lust. It comes on those what 'ave taken the Jollop.'

'What do you mean?'

'A desire for cheese, a mad craving. The cheese lust!'

'Are you sure?'

'Yes. Old Snatcher has been working on it for years. He found some old book of cheese fables in his collection and started researching it. He found more and more stories about some plant that had wonderful effects on illnesses but cursed those that it cured with the cheese lust. So he got hold of some of this plant and set about his experiments. He was dosing up all kinds of animals with stuff and most of them went bonkers. But his favourite was the dogs. Once he dosed them up they made the best cheese hounds, but right vicious. We had to keep them muzzled. They would do anything for a whiff of cheese. Then a while ago he had a bit of a run in with you lot and he had to start out again. He had the bright idea that if could get everybody to take the stuff there would be so much demand for cheese that it would have to be decriminalized and he would get rich in the cheese trade again.'

'And the Spa was just a way to get people to take this evil substance?'

'Once he dosed them up they made the best cheese hounds, but right vicious'

'You got it right. Now give me the sandwich!'

'Just one last thing. Are we off to collect more of this plant he needs, then?'

'Yes, it only grows on one island on the whole planet.'

Willbury threw the sandwich on the floor in disgust. 'Let him have it.'

Fingle's guard released him, and the man fell upon the sandwich. In a trice it was gone.

'What shall we do with him now?'

'Lock him in the bilges.'

Fingle was taken off and those that remained stood in silence. Snatcher had again proved himself the most evil of men.

'I suggest we turn the ship about right away,' said Willbury. 'We cannot countenance delivering more of this evil substance to our fair country.'

'Hear! Hear!'

Then it struck Arthur. HIS GRANDFATHER HAD BEEN POISONED!

'Grandfather! What are we going to do? He's been poisoned! We have to cure him!'

'I'm not sure what we can do.' The realization of what they had just learnt was sinking in, and the group looked miserable.

'There may not be a cure,' Arthur muttered. 'Then what?'

'Ask Snatcher?' said Kipper who had joined them. 'We have got him in a bit of a corner.'

'I doubt he is going to help us with this. But we can try.'

'What else can we do?' said Willbury.

'I've a few ideas,' Bert added darkly.

They trooped up to the stern and used the stick to knock on the window of the cabin below. A very sleepy face looked out through the window.

'What is it?'

'We want to speak to Snatcher.'

'I'll go and get him.'

Snatcher appeared. 'What do you want now?'

Willbury looked down in contempt. 'We know what you have been up to with your Black Jollop.'

Snatcher looked startled. 'How? You been spying through walls?'

'Never you mind. We know everything. Your poisoning of the ill, the cheese lust, and how you intended to start up the cheese trade again.'

'Blooming Henry! You do know it all.' Then a dark look crossed his face. 'It was that Fingle. I'll have 'im.'

'It was that Fingle. I'll have 'im.'

'Never mind that. We need you to help us cure everybody.'

'You must be joking. Even if I end up back in prison, when I get out the demand for cheese will still be so high it will be easy to get it legalized again. That Jollop is permanent. That is the beauty of it. So many have taken the cure that using my cheese knowledge and contacts I will come the richest man in the land.'

Marjorie spoke. 'You are disgusting!'

Snatcher just laughed.

'And there is no cure for the cheese lust?'

'NO!' Snatcher scoffed.

All the windows of the captain's cabin were now open and filled with heads.

'You will never profit by this. I will make sure that you and that doctor of yours will never get out of prison.'

'Even if I have to live out my days in jail, just the thought of that cheesy desire will be enough to keep me going,' snapped Snatcher. 'It's a very sweet revenge for what Ratbridge has done to me.'

'You're mad!' said Willbury and Snatcher rolled his eyes.

Marjorie noticed that the doctor had been watching all that had been going on and seemed to be trying to catch her attention without being noticed by Snatcher.

When he saw that Marjorie had seen him he clearly mouthed 'I can help'. She turned and led the group away from the rail.

 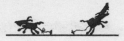

'I think the doctor wants to talk to us. He was signalling to me when Willbury was talking to Snatcher.'

'Wants to save his own skin.'

'Maybe, but why would he be signalling to me?' Marjorie wondered.

'Let's find out. Ask him.'

'Don't do that. If he's down there, and turns on Snatcher, Snatcher will do him in. No. We have to get him out somehow.'

'How do we do that?' asked Kipper.

'He's a doctor, isn't he. Tell Snatcher that someone is ill and needs a doctor,' suggested Arthur.

'Brilliant idea.'

They returned to the rail.

'We want a favour from you.'

'Do you really!' laughed Snatcher.

'Yes. We need a doctor. One of the crew has got a very large boil.'

'I am glad to hear it. Why should I help you lot?'

'I might go a little easier on you in court if you show some compassion,' answered Willbury.

Snatcher weighed up the situation. 'Very well. You are welcome to him. Fat lot of good it will do you. He is useless as a doctor. When I found him he was reduced to working as a receptionist at a vet's.'

The crew lowered a rope and hauled up the doctor. As soon as he was over the rail he spoke.

'There isn't a real boil, is there? I can't stand them. They make me go funny just looking at them.'

'No. No. Why were you trying to get my attention?'

The doctor looked round at Willbury. 'If I can help you will you drop charges against me?'

Willbury looked distrustful. 'It would have to be some very real help, and I still might not be able to promise you anything. But remember if you don't it could be life in clink!'

'Well, I think there might be a cure for the cheese lust.'

'There isn't a real boil is there?'

'In my spare time I'd do hair-related experiments'

Chapter 10

THE DOCTOR'S STORY

'I didn't start out with the intention of being a crook. My father was a doctor, as was his father before him, and my mother had her heart set on me being one as well. I started my medical training in Edinburgh and at first it went very well. Then I fell in with what I can only call "a bad set".

'I'd developed an interest in hair and everything about it. The chemical composition of different colours, the way it grew, how to make it grow, everything! I still find it fascinating. In my spare time I'd do hair-related experiments and slowly my experiments took over my life. I stopped attending lectures and seldom went out apart from to the barbers to collect sweepings. I became more and more obsessed with male early-onset baldness. I knew if I could understand it I might be able to find a cure and that would make my name and fortune.

'In the early autumn of my third year I discovered certain chemical changes in the scalps and hair of those becoming rapidly bald and I knew I was on to something. But there was a problem. I needed hair samples and I needed them from the very men who least liked giving it up. Those going prematurely bald!

'In my desperation I turned to drink and one night in a bar I met two very unsavoury characters. I fell into conversation with them and told them about my work. Strangely they seemed very interested, and after a few more drinks said they might be able to help me with my studies. I asked how as they both had a very full head of hair and they told me it was better not to ask. Before I left I gave them my card and thought nothing more of it.

'Then a few days later there was a knock at my door. I was surprised, but as the rent wasn't due I answered it. Before me were the men I'd met in the bar.

'I wasn't sure why they had come to visit me, and not having had a drink they seemed even less appealing. I asked them what they wanted and they told me they had something for me.'

'What was it?' asked Arthur.

'Fresh hair from a balding man! They produced a small folded piece of newspaper and unwrapped it to reveal a pile of fine ginger hair. Now I've not mentioned this, but ginger hair is the highest in the chemicals I was seeking so my delight was intense and I offered to pay the men well. The men then said that the hair was a free sample, and more could be provided whenever I wanted. With that they left their cards and were gone.'

'They produced a small folded piece of newspaper and unwrapped it to reveal a pile of fine ginger hair'

Willbury had raised a hand. 'Sir, let me ask you their names?'

The doctor looked ashamed. 'Their names, sir, were Broadwood and Widger.'

'I thought they might be.'

Arthur was astonished that Willbury knew the names of the men and was about to ask how, but Willbury signalled to him to stay quiet and allow the doctor to continue his story.

'I was very thankful for this supply of new hair and it proved to be the best sample I had ever analysed. But soon it was gone in the flurry of experiments that it allowed. So I went to see Mr Broadwood. I found him at home in a small but luxurious house not too far from the centre of the city. When he saw me at the door he pulled me in quickly and then offered me tea.

'"I suppose you need more hair?" he asked.

'I admitted that this was indeed why I'd come and asked if he could supply me again. He replied that he could but this time there would be a cost. Fourteen groats was the sum. A huge amount in those days, but I had my allowance from my parents so I agreed.

'A few days later the hair arrived and again it was of beautiful quality. I worked for several days and again the hair was used up. So again I visited Broadwood.

'Over the next few weeks I spent more than two hundred groats, just on hair. But *what* hair! My experiments were starting to bear fruit and then . . . it happened.

'Needing more hair, I set off late one evening to collect another batch from Broadwood. As I left his house I can only have walked a few yards when I suddenly felt a hand on my collar.

'"I am arresting you under the 1738 Trading in Illegally Gathered Scalps and Toenail Act."

'Oh, the shame of it! I was being arrested by members of the Edinburgh hair robbery squad. Deep down I knew that the hair I had been using must have been collected illegally but I had swept those thoughts away with the wonder of my scientific experiments.

'I was being arrested by members of the Edinburgh hair robbery squad'

'So yes, you guessed correctly Mr Nibble. Broadwood and Widger, the infamous hair robbers, had been my suppliers. They would go out at night, find drunken balding men, offer them spiked drinks and then when the men passed out shave off their last remaining hair.

'They got twenty years and transportation, while my family got me a very good lawyer and I got off with a ten groat fine and barring from the medical profession. After the trial my family cut off my allowance and disowned me. So I moved south and hid myself in the "job" that Snatcher mentioned. A receptionist at a vet's practice. That is where he found me.'

'What on earth was Snatcher doing going to a vet's?' asked Arthur.

'He turned up and asked if we had any spare animals. Thinking he was after something as a pet, I told him that the animals we had were mostly ill or very old. To my surprise this seemed to be exactly what he wanted. Then I asked him what type of animal he wanted and he said everything we had. At the vet's we always like to give homes to animals if we can so I offered to find out what we had and told him I could run them round to him later.

'When I turned up with the animals, my interest was raised when I saw much of the same equipment I had been using in my own experiment. I asked him about his work and we talked for hours about complex organic molecules and such things. Around midnight I made to leave and he asked me if I wanted a job. With no hesitation I said yes and the next day I started to help him with his work.'

'What were you doing?' asked Marjorie.

'Each day plants in parcels from around the world would turn up and we would crush them up and analyse them. He told me he was trying to find a fabled plant whose extract could cure almost all ills but which also had some very interesting side effects.'

'We would crush them up and analyse them'

'Who sent the plants?'

'Snatcher placed adverts in botanical magazines right

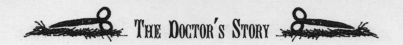
across the world. Thousands of samples came in but most had no healing effect at all.'

'How did you know?'

'We tested them on animals, usually with no effect . . . or at least no positive effect. But one day a package arrived with the seeds of a tree from the rainforests of some Pacific island. They were not like any I'd seen before, and when tested we found they were rich in new chemical compounds. Snatcher made up some pills from the refined compounds and fed it to a tiny puppy. The puppy hadn't been well but very, very quickly—in fact within a number of minutes—it was bright and breezy as anything.

'Snatcher kept the puppy under a close watch and on the third day noticed the dog was sniffing the air at lunchtime. From the larder Snatcher took a covered dish and lifted the lid. The very moment he did the little dog attacked him savagely. But instead of Snatcher being cross he seemed very happy. I didn't discover what had been in that dish until later.

'Instead of Snatcher being cross he seemed very happy'

'So we'd discovered a fabled cure. He wrote to the plant collector who'd forwarded the parcel to us and soon a much larger package arrived. We set about refining its contents and making a syrup so we could control the dosages.

'I did ask him about the behaviour of the puppy and he told me not to worry. I know now that it was the side effects that he wanted to exploit.

'Then we started human trials. The results were remarkable. No illness seemed able to resist our Black Jollop. Our patients were people Snatcher found in the villages around Ratbridge. After a few days one or two of them came back and Snatcher would see them alone. After these consultations the patient left contented so I left it at that.'

'And how did you learn the truth about the side effects?'

'One morning when I was working alone and I found a book on the work bench in our laboratory. There was a marker in its pages. So I sat with a cup of tea and read. The volume was a book of fairytales and legends featuring cheese.

'The volume was a book of fairytale and legends featuring cheese'

'Amongst the stories I found one that told of a distant island where a giant cabbage grew. Under its shade lived a happy people who used the tree for medicine, but found that it also made them crazy for cheese.'

The doctor turned to Marjorie. 'The point is, in the story the people took another plant to save them from the madness. So there might be a cure.'

'But that is just a storybook.'

'Yes, but it is that very same legend that told of our original plant as well.'

'True. I think you might have something,' said Marjorie.

'And you knew of the terrible side effect and still went along with Snatcher's plan. That is truly appalling,' Willbury snapped angrily at the Doctor.

'Yes. I'm afraid so. I just couldn't face the idea of returning to the vet's, so I kept my mouth closed and went along with him. As part of his plan there was the spa and I was given centre stage. I just couldn't resist it.'

'You are a truly awful man. You went along with Snatcher and his scheme knowing that it might be causing people harm. Shocking! Didn't you swear the Hippocratic oath?' Willbury asked.

The doctor dropped his gaze to the floor, looking very ashamed.

Arthur had listened very hard and now wanted an answer to his own question. 'So you think that the plant in the story that cures the lust is real?'

'Yes I do. It all adds up.'

'In evolution there is quite often a symbiotic relationship between one organism that is poisonous and another that has learnt to live alongside it that produces an antidote or anti-venom,' added Marjorie.

'Well, if that is the case I guess we have to go to the island to see if we can find the cure.'

'No doubt about it.'

The doctor then looked a little worried. 'What do you want me to do?'

'I think you'd better join Fingle in the bilges. Snatcher is going to wonder why we are still heading towards the island and may guess you've told us something.'

As the doctor was taken off Arthur spoke to Marjorie. 'Do you think it's true?'

'Yes I do. Now all we have to do is find that island.'

'Now all we have to do is find that island'

NOGENS SENTENTIA PRO IGNARUS

SNAP·STOP·TROTTING·
BADGER·PACIFIER·

1 GROAT

·Ratbridge·Gazette·

Cheese Conservationists Bring In New Breeding Stock!

Members of the RWCA are bringing in new cheeses to help rebuild the local population. We applaud this move, but ask 'Will our cheeses be the same?'

'The cheeses we're importing are from South Wales and while paler and not so well scented, are close biological cousins of our local cheeses and should breed easily with them.'

The sea became very rough

Chapter 11

SOUTH TO THE HORN

Even running with full sail and the boiler steaming twenty-four hours a day, it took another week for the ship to reach Cape Horn. As the ship sailed south, it became colder, and colder, and the sea became very rough. Arthur had not really thought very much about how the ship might hold up to high winds and weather, but now he was amazed by how well she coped with the huge rolling seas. The crew were also showing what fine sailors they were under their captain Tom.

As the weather worsened it became increasingly difficult to work out their position. There was no sun for Marjorie to make a reading from, and but she knew they must be very close to the coast of Patagonia. She was constantly nervous and jumpy, as there was the danger that they could run aground at any time, and frustratingly little she could do to make sure they stayed safe.

Then came an albatross. The crew spotted her gliding just feet over the surface of the giant rollers. Soon she was flying alongside them, barely moving her vast wings as she did.

Gliding just feet over the surface of the giant rollers

'Bit windy, isn't it!' she called.

'Yes!' shouted Tom through cupped hands.

'We must be mad to be out in this!'

'Yes!' yelled Tom again.

'Where are you going?'

'To the Pacific—we hope. We haven't been able to get a good bearing because of the weather.'

'Yes, it's terrible. Always is around here.'

'And I thought the weather in England was bad,' muttered Kipper from under his sou'wester. The wind was so strong now that it felt as if it was blowing the rain right into his skin.

'Well, must love you and leave you!' called the albatross cheerily. With the tiniest movement of her wings, she wheeled to the right and started to swoop out across the waves.

Marjorie looked up suddenly from the chart she was studying. 'Before you go!' she shouted after the disappearing bird.

For a moment it seemed as if Marjorie's call would be lost in the wind, but then the albatross glided back round towards them.

'Yes?'

'Are we going in the right direction?'

'No.'

'WHAT!'

'No, you want to go directly south for about fifty miles. Otherwise you'll bump into land.'

'OH!' shouted Marjorie, looking rather stunned. 'Thank you!'

'No problem. Have a nice day!' And with that the albatross was off over the waves and gone.

Tom turned the ship directly south guided by the compass on the bridge, and they sailed on until Marjorie thought it was safe to turn west.

Tom turned the ship directly south

A day later the weather finally cleared enough for Marjorie to take a reading and she announced they were indeed in the Pacific and it would be safe to head north-west towards their destination.

Arthur spent most of his time with Willbury below deck, as the rolling seas and strong winds had grown very tiring, but to everybody's surprise Fish was now spending every moment he could on deck. It didn't matter what the weather was like. Fish was always there. And when he was not by the wheel he was to be seen standing on the bow and leaning into the wind. He seemed to have fallen in love with the ocean. When Kipper had first noticed this he disappeared for a few hours and returned on deck with an oilskin box cover he'd made for Fish. This Fish now wore proudly as he took on the elements.

He was to be seen standing on the bow and leaning into the wind

Onwards they ran and the weather became better with each mile further north they travelled. Marjorie spent a lot of time looking at the maps as she was trying to make sure they wouldn't miss the small island. Then one evening she came to Tom as he stood by the wheel.

'I think that we'll be in sight of the island by tomorrow afternoon.'

'Good,' said Tom. 'Just in time too as we've almost run out of fuel. I've enjoyed being back at sea, but I shall be very happy to have my feet on solid earth again.'

'Have you thought what we're going to do with Snatcher and his mob when we get there?'

'Yes . . . they're a real problem. But it's not just them. What about the trotting badgers?'

'I know. Once we're in shallow waters within reach of the island, Snatcher and his mob will be able to escape out of the window. It might be better to get them somewhere we can keep them under guard,' suggested Marjorie.

'We could stick them under the forecastle where we store the sails!'

'That would work. There are no windows in the sail store,' agreed Marjorie.

Tom rubbed his head. 'There is still the problem of getting them out of their cabin and up here. The trotting badgers are blocking the stairs to the cabin.'

'We could haul them up in the net over the stern.'

'I think you have forgotten one thing. Snatcher's men still

have their weapons,' said Tom. 'And I doubt they'll agree to just giving them up and becoming our prisoners.'

Bert had been listening and suddenly perked up. 'Well, there may be a way round that.'

'What?' asked Kipper.

'What?' asked Kipper

'Remember that old saying about keeping your powder dry? Let's get out the hose and power up the bilge pump again.'

'You mean dampen their ardour!' giggled Marjorie.

'Not half,' chuckled Bert.

'I don't understand?' asked Tom.

'If we can get their gunpowder wet, their guns will be useless.'

'But they're down below and we're up here. How do we get their gunpowder wet?'

'Holes!'

'What do you mean?'

'Get Kipper and Arthur up here and have them sort out the pump and hose. I'll go and get me toolkit.'

By the time Bert returned to the bridge, Kipper and Arthur were dragging the end of the hose up from the deck. Bert opened his toolbox and took out a bit and brace.

'This should do the trick.' He started to drill holes through the planking of the bridge, down through the ceiling of the captain's cabin.

He started to drill holes through the planking

'We can block these holes up with corks and tar later.'

The wood of the deck was thick and very hard but after an hour there were about twenty holes spread over the deck.

'Start the pump!' shouted Bert as he pushed the hose into the first of the holes.

'Start the pump!'

Arthur heard cries from below as the water shot down into the cabin.

'Have to move it about a bit and surprise them. We need to get everything nice and wet down there,' said Bert as he jumped from hole to hole with the hose. After about ten minutes of screaming from below even Bert thought that it had probably worked.

'Turn off the pump. I think their ardour is sufficiently dampened.'

Marjorie took the long stick and knocked on the cabin window. A very wet and disgruntled Snatcher appeared.

'What was that for?'

'Thought you might need a wash,' laughed Bert.

Snatcher gave Bert a very nasty look but didn't say anything.

Now that Snatcher was suitably softened up Marjorie spoke. 'We are offering you the chance to co-operate with us.'

'And if we don't?'

'Would you like another wash?'

'NO! We'll co-operate.'

'OK. We'll haul you all up and put you somewhere safe away from the badgers. If you don't try anything we won't harm you.'

Bert and a lot of the larger crew members had armed themselves with old swords and clubs, and acted as guards as Snatcher and his men were lifted up over the stern and escorted to the sail store. Once the prisoners were inside the door was bolted and locked.

As night fell the sky cleared and a warm westerly breeze came up.

'We are all set for the island,' said Marjorie as she finished taking a reading from the Southern Cross.

Escorted to the sail store

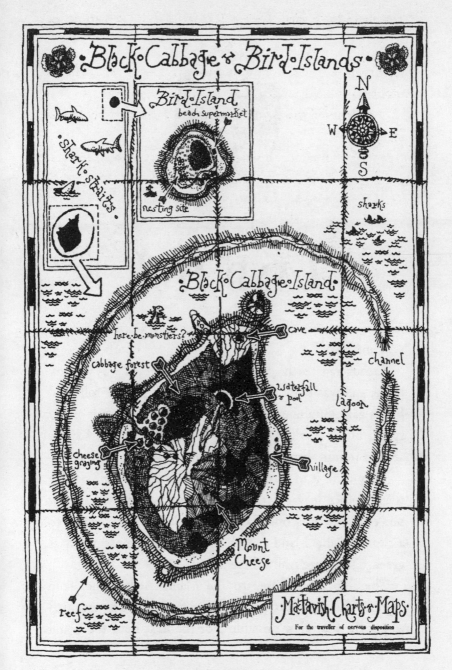

· Black · Cabbage & Bird · Islands ·

· Shark · straits ·

Bird · Island
beach supermarket

nesting site

N
W   E
S

sharks

· Black · Cabbage · Island ·

here · be · monsters?

cave

channel

cabbage forest

waterfall & pool

lagoon

cheese grazing

village

Mount Cheese

reef

· MacTavish · Charts & Maps ·
For the traveller of nervous disposition

Arthur followed Fish's gaze and saw a tiny speck

Chapter 12

LAND HO!

At first light there was a cry from the masthead.

'Land ho!'

Arthur ran to the forecastle to look. Fish was already there, and was pointing into the distance. Arthur followed Fish's gaze. Straining to see, he could just make out a tiny speck, but it was too far away to see what it was. Kipper arrived to join them carrying a large telescope.

They took it in turns to have a look at the approaching island. When it was Arthur's turn he was surprised at how powerful the telescope was. The speck was transformed to a clearly visible island and he could see that most of it was green. They were really there at last!

The ship drew closer to the island. Arthur and Tom climbed the rigging to get to the crow's nest. They wanted to get the best view possible. For the next hour the island

grew bigger. As they got closer Arthur could see waves rising and breaking some distance from the island.

'Why are the waves breaking before they reach the island?'

'Quite often there is a ring of coral that runs around islands. It's called a reef and the waves break when they hit it,' said Tom.

'Well, how do we get to the island then?'

'If the sea bed is uneven there can be a break in the reef. We'll have to look out for one, as there may only be one place we can get through.'

Arthur scanned the breaking waves and saw that there was indeed a place where the waves didn't seem to be breaking. He pointed it out to Tom.

'There!'

'Very good, Arthur.' Tom called down to the deck. 'There is a break in the reef.'

'There is a break in the reef.'

'What direction?' called back Kipper, who was now on the wheel.

'Ten degrees to starboard.'

Kipper changed course and made for the passage.

Then Arthur spotted two of the crew on the forecastle, each dropping weights on ropes on either side of the bow.

'What are they doing?'

'Checking the depth of the water,' said Tom. 'We don't know these waters and could run aground. The ropes have knots in them six feet apart. Six feet is called a fathom, and they call out the number of fathoms when the weight hits the sea bed.'

He watched the sailors checking how much line they were paying out each time they dropped the weights, then calling back to Kipper.

Kipper continued steering the ship towards the break and instructed the crew to lower some of the sails.

At about a hundred yards from the break Kipper ordered the rest of the sails to be dropped. The ship slowed and slid smoothly through the gap in the reef. From Arthur's position up in the crow's nest he could see the reef under the water, stretching out in a ring parallel to the beach. Inside the reef the waters became very calm and the ship moved almost silently towards the shore.

Arthur looked towards the island. A thick green canopy started after a wide sandy beach. Arthur gazed into the jungle. Somewhere in there was the plant they needed! Arthur felt a bubble of excitement start up inside him. At last it seemed that they would really be able to find the

antidote and cure everyone who had been poisoned by the Black Jollop—including Grandfather!

As the ship drew closer into land, more and more of the crew gathered on the deck below them.

'I think we had better get down there too,' said Tom. 'We don't want to be last in.'

'Last in?'

'Yes, as soon as the anchor is dropped, anybody who hasn't got a job to do has to jump in the sea. It's a bit of a tradition.'

The ship had slowed almost to a stop a few hundred yards from the beach when Kipper called for the anchor to be dropped. As the anchor found a hold on the seabed the ship slowly swung its bow into the wind and came to rest. Then there was a cry.

'Last one in is a mouldy old goat!'

Arthur and Tom were still some way up the rigging when the cry went out, and they stopped for a moment to watch as bodies flung themselves over the side.

'I think we'd better jump from here if we're not to be last in,' said Tom.

He then took a leap and shouted 'Geronimo!' as he plummeted into the bright blue water. Arthur was not so sure. He kept climbing down, trying to pluck up the courage to jump.

'Come on, Arthur!' shouted Tom. 'There's hardly anyone left to jump!'

Screwing up his courage, Arthur leapt and, following Tom's lead, shouted 'Geronimo'. He hit the water and was surprised at how warm it was. As he surfaced he saw the faces of friends all around him.

Then somebody shouted. 'Kipper is an old goat!'

Everybody in the water turned to look. Kipper had appeared in a strange orange and blue knitted bathing suit and was about to jump from the side of the ship.

'Always last.' It was Tom, who was a few feet from Arthur in the water.

Kipper jumped and there was another cheer. Then Arthur noticed Fish standing on the handrail at the side of the ship. He couldn't believe his eyes. The boxtroll jumped!

For a second the boxtroll disappeared below the water but then bobbed straight to the surface.

'I can't believe it!'

Tom spoke. 'Thought that would surprise you. Kipper filled all the spare space inside his box with corks. Now he will float like one.'

Arthur laughed and swam over to Fish. He had never seen Fish look so happy. The boxtroll was now paddling around gurgling and wailing with joy, and even splashed at Arthur as he came close.

'You've changed!'

Fish nodded and splashed some more.

'Very good Fish. You really are living up to your name,' Willbury called from the rail of the ship.

He had never seen Fish look so happy

'Come on in and join us,' Arthur called back.

'No, no, no. I shall leave it to you young ones to enjoy the waters. I had a good wash this morning.'

'When do we go ashore?' Arthur asked Tom.

'I think we'll leave it until tomorrow. It mightn't be wise to go into the jungle just as it gets dark.'

As the sun went down the crew set fishing lines off the sides of the ship and soon had enough for supper. The boiler still had enough heat in it to cook the fish and in a few minutes everybody was tucking in. The crew even passed some through the bars to Snatcher and his mob.

The boiler still had enough heat in it to cook the fish

Arthur sat with Willbury and Fish as they tucked in.

'Be interesting to see what happens tomorrow.'

'Yes, Arthur. I hope we do find the plants we are looking for. There is a chance we won't. God alone knows what's on that island.'

This they were to discover first thing the following morning. The night had been very dark but as the sun broke over the horizon it silhouetted the shape of a huge lizard walking towards the ship.

On deck Kipper and Bert saw it at the same time and let out a huge scream.

'WHAT IS IT?'

The monster moved closer.

'WHAT IS IT?'

1 GROAT

·THE· ·Ratbridge·Gazette·

Welsh Cheeses Eaten!

This morning tearful members of the RWCA reported that all imported Welsh cheeses seem to have been eaten.

'It seems they were easy prey. Even though they have not fared so well in recent times our local cheeses have a certain cunning and speed. The Welsh cheeses were pale and rather weak so were very vulnerable. When our newly appointed cheese warden went out to inspect them this morning there were none left.'

When asked what was to be the next move to save our cheeses, the RWCA spokesman shrugged his shoulders and muttered that they might have to consider stronger foreign cheeses.

This paper says, 'DO WE WANT FOREIGN CHEESE?'

'You've got to get out!'

Chapter 13

MONSTER!

The monster was huge . . . and coming straight towards them. Everyone started panicking.

'What are we going to do?'

'I . . . I don't know. That thing is coming straight at us and it doesn't look friendly.'

'Load up the cannon?'

'It would be like firing a peashooter at an elephant!'

'How about every man for himself! Swim for the shore!'

'Is swimming for the shore a good idea?' asked Marjorie. 'That monster has come from the island, after all—who knows what else might be lurking on there?'

Tom looked thoughtful. 'You are right . . . but I don't think we have any choice! If we stay on the ship we are just sitting ducks. I'm going to give the order to make for the island.'

'What about Snatcher and his men?' pointed out Arthur.

'They're locked in the sail store.'

Everyone looked at the door. There was no time to think.

'I think we had better let them out? If not . . . '

'Are you sure you don't just want to leave them to their fate?' Bert asked.

'No. We can't be that heartless. Let them out.'

Reluctantly Bert unlocked the door.

'You've got to get out!'

'Why?'

'There's a monster about to attack us. If you want to save yourselves swim for the shore.'

It took a few moments for the news to sink in and then Snatcher spoke again.

'I don't believe you.'

'All of you! Come out here and have a look.'

They did as they were told and looked towards where the crew were staring.

'Blooming Henry! Swim for your lives!'

A stream of Snatcher's men followed him over the side and started to make for the beach.

'OK! Abandon ship!' ordered Tom. 'And Kipper, you'd better go and let Fingle and the doctor free.'

Kipper rushed below deck, returned with the bilge residents, and with rather too much enthusiasm 'helped' them over the side.

Arthur felt a hand on his shoulder.

'I can't swim.' It was Willbury.

Arthur looked about the deck for something that would float and spotted the apple barrel.

'Kipper, Marjorie! Give me a hand.'

They managed to roll the barrel across the deck and lower it over the side so it floated mouth up in the water. Then they helped Willbury climb down and into the barrel.

'We'll be able to push him along with us.'

'OK,' shouted Kipper, and joined Arthur and the others as they jumped into the sea.

'Push!'

Arthur looked towards the monster. It was only about 200 yards from the ship and closing fast. The barrel was moving very slowly.

'Push harder!' he cried.

'Push harder!'

'Thank you for saving me,' came a weak voice from inside the barrel.

No one was left on the ship apart from the trotting badgers, but the sea was filled with very energetic swimmers. Between strokes everybody was keeping an eye on the lumbering monster.

It reached the ship and stopped. Its enormous eyes scanned the decks. Then it slowly looked to left and right in the sea.

'It's seen us!'

Arthur watched as the enormous head turned towards them. It opened its huge wide mouth and revealed tombstone-sized teeth.

Screaming mixed with the sound of the waves.

It opened its huge wide mouth and revealed tombstone-sized teeth.

What Happens Next . . .

In book 3, *Cheezilla!*, the *Nautical Laundry* must reach Black Cabbage Island to find the antidote to the poisonous side effects of Black Jollop.

Without it, the town will forever be consumed by the cheese lust . . . but first the crew must get past the monster on-shore!

Read the next thrilling instalment of *Worse Things Happen at Sea!* to discover the answers to all these questions and more . . .

What happens when the helpless crew is swallowed by the monster . . .

. . . and how will they manage to escape?

Why is the rain on the island so dangerous?

Just what else does Snatcher have up his sleeves?

And what is so important about a smelly sock,

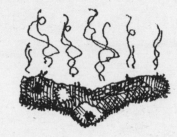

a most unusual mixture,

and a very cheesy disguise?

Book 3,
Cheezilla!,
available now!
ISBN 978-0-19-279274-7

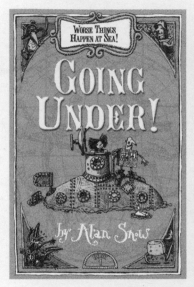

Join Arthur and his friends in the first
wonderfully weird Ratbridge Chronicles
adventure, HERE BE MONSTERS!

Book 1

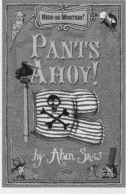

ISBN 978-0-19-275540-7

Book 2

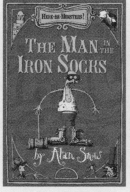

ISBN 978-0-19-275541-4

Book 3

ISBN 978-0-19-275542-1

Beneath the streets of Ratbridge, something is
stirring ... It is up to Arthur, prevented from going
home by the evil Snatcher, to save the day.
With the help of Willbury Nibble QC (retired),
a band of boxtrolls, some cabbageheads, and Marjorie
the inventor, can Arthur keep Ratbridge from
danger—and find his way home?

www.ratbridgechronicles.com

Come in and explore the wonderful world of
Ratbridge at our RATBRIDGE CHRONICLES! website.
You'll find all sorts of bits and bobs to keep you as
happy as a boxtroll in a pile of nuts and bolts.

Look out for competitions, games,
screensavers, maps, and much, much more!

Alan Snow is a well-known author and
illustrator of children's books, and has also
worked in many fields of design and animation.

WORSE THINGS HAPPEN AT SEA! is his second story
set in the wonderfully weird world of Ratbridge,
and follows HERE BE MONSTERS!